HIP-HOP

Alicia Keys
Ashanti
Beyoncé
Black Eyed Peas
Busta Rhymes
Chris Brown
Christina Aguilera
Ciara
Cypress Hill
Daddy Yankee
DMX
Don Omar
Dr. Dre
Eminem
Fat Joe
50 Cent
The Game
Hip-Hop: A Short History
Hip-Hop Around the World
Ice Cube
Ivy Queen
Jay-Z
Jennifer Lopez
Juelz Santana
Kanye West
Lil' Wayne
LL Cool J
Lloyd Banks
Ludacris
Mariah Carey
Mary J. Blige
Missy Elliot
Nas
Nelly
Notorious B.I.G.
Outkast
Pharrell Williams
Pitbull
Queen Latifah
Reverend Run (of Run DMC)
Sean "Diddy" Combs
Snoop Dogg
T.I.
Tupac
Usher
Will Smith
Wu-Tang Clan
Xzibit
Young Jeezy
Yung Joc

The Game has worked hard to go from drug dealer to music icon. It has been—and continues to be—a journey with many ups and downs.

The Game

Lindsey Sanna

Mason Crest Publishers

The Game

Produced by Harding House Publishing Service, Inc.
201 Harding Avenue, Vestal, NY 13850.

MASON CREST PUBLISHERS INC.
370 Reed Road
Broomall, Pennsylvania 19008
(866)MCP-BOOK (toll free)
www.masoncrest.com

Printed in the United States of America

First Printing

9 8 7 6 5 4 3 2 1

Library of Congress Cataloging-in-Publication Data

Sanna, Lindsey.
The Game / Lindsey Sanna.
p. cm. — (Hip-hop)
Includes index.
ISBN-13: 978-1-4222-0292-0
ISBN-13: 978-1-4222-0077-3 (series)
1. Game (Musician)—Juvenile literature. 2. Rap musicians—United States—Biography—Juvenile literature. I. Title.
ML3930.G22S36 2008
782.42164092—dc22

2007028140

Publisher's notes:

- All quotations in this book come from original sources and contain the spelling and grammatical inconsistencies of the original text.

- The Web sites mentioned in this book were active at the time of publication. The publisher is not responsible for Web sites that have changed their addresses or discontinued operation since the date of publication. The publisher will review and update the Web site addresses each time the book is reprinted.

DISCLAIMER: The following story has been thoroughly researched, and to the best of our knowledge, represents a true story. While every possible effort has been made to ensure accuracy, the publisher will not assume liability for damages caused by inaccuracies in the data, and makes no warranty on the accuracy of the information contained herein. This story has not been authorized nor endorsed by The Game.

Contents

Hip-Hop Time Line

1970

1980

1970s DJ Kool Herc pioneers the use of breaks, isolations, and repeats using two turntables.

1970s Grafitti artist Vic begins tagging on New York subways.

1970s The central elements of the hip-hop culture begin to emerge in the Bronx, New York City.

1974 Afrika Bambaataa organizes the Universal Zulu Nation.

1976 Grandmaster Flash and the Furious Five emerge as one of the first battlers and freestylers.

1979 "Rapper's Delight," by The Sugarhill Gang, goes gold.

1980 Rapper Kurtis Blow sells a million records and makes the first nationwide TV appearance for a hip-hop artist.

1981 Grandmaster Flash and the Furious Five release *Adventures on the Wheels of Steel*.

1982 Afrika Bambaataa tours Europe in another hip-hop first.

1983 Ice-T releases his first singles, marking the earliest examples of gangsta rap.

1984 The track "Roxanne Roxanne" sparks the first diss war.

1984 *Graffitti Rock*, the first hip-hop television program, premieres.

1985 The film *Krush Groove*, about the rise of Def Jam Records, is released.

1986 Run DMC cover Aerosmith's "Walk this Way" and appear on the cover of *Rolling Stone*.

1988 Hip-hop record sales reach 100 million annually.

1988 MTV premieres *Yo! MTV Raps*.

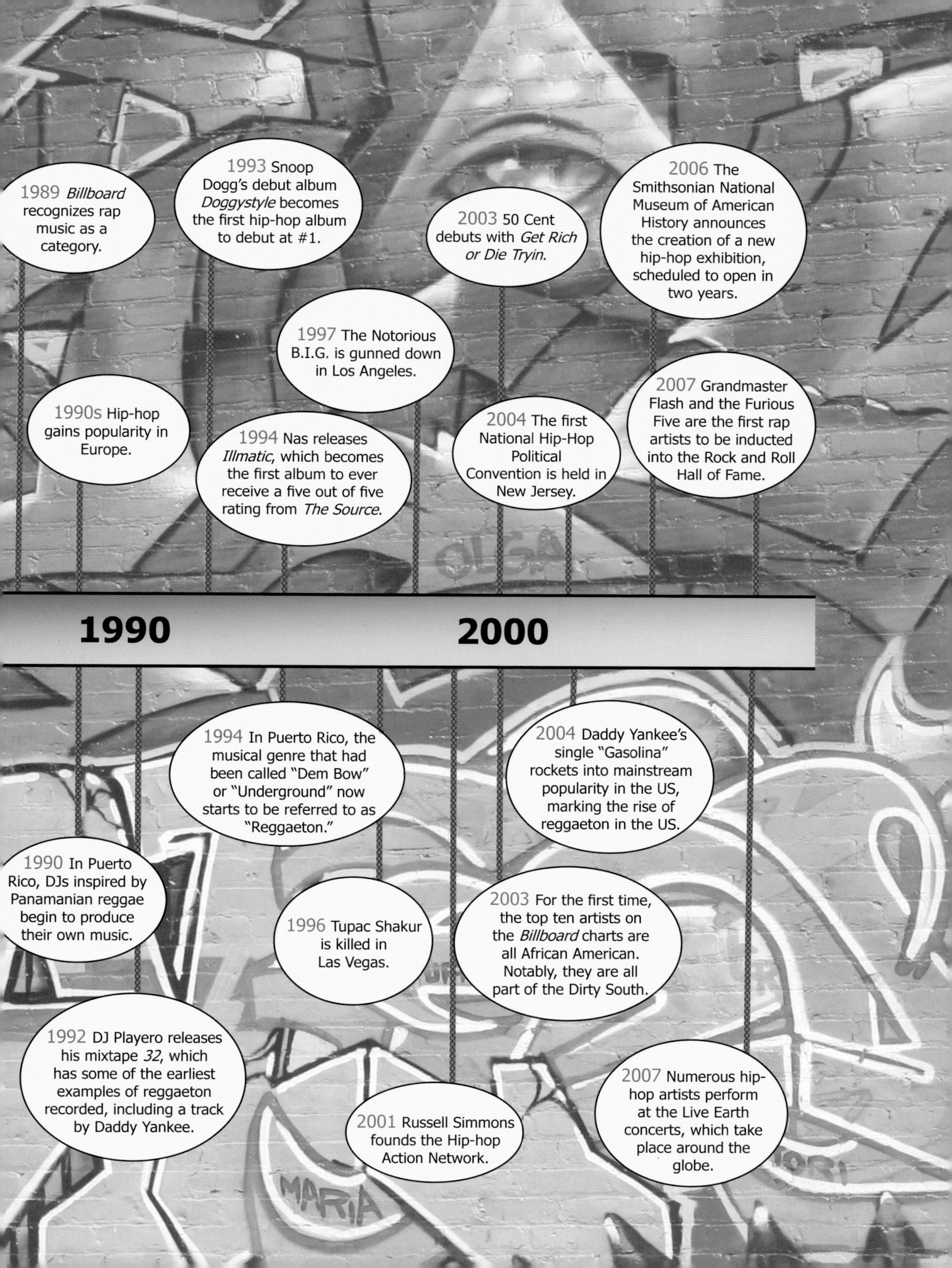
1989 *Billboard* recognizes rap music as a category.
1993 Snoop Dogg's debut album *Doggystyle* becomes the first hip-hop album to debut at #1.
2003 50 Cent debuts with *Get Rich or Die Tryin*.
2006 The Smithsonian National Museum of American History announces the creation of a new hip-hop exhibition, scheduled to open in two years.
1997 The Notorious B.I.G. is gunned down in Los Angeles.
1990s Hip-hop gains popularity in Europe.
1994 Nas releases *Illmatic*, which becomes the first album to ever receive a five out of five rating from *The Source*.
2004 The first National Hip-Hop Political Convention is held in New Jersey.
2007 Grandmaster Flash and the Furious Five are the first rap artists to be inducted into the Rock and Roll Hall of Fame.
1990
2000
1994 In Puerto Rico, the musical genre that had been called "Dem Bow" or "Underground" now starts to be referred to as "Reggaeton."
2004 Daddy Yankee's single "Gasolina" rockets into mainstream popularity in the US, marking the rise of reggaeton in the US.
1990 In Puerto Rico, DJs inspired by Panamanian reggae begin to produce their own music.
1996 Tupac Shakur is killed in Las Vegas.
2003 For the first time, the top ten artists on the *Billboard* charts are all African American. Notably, they are all part of the Dirty South.
1992 DJ Playero releases his mixtape *32*, which has some of the earliest examples of reggaeton recorded, including a track by Daddy Yankee.
2001 Russell Simmons founds the Hip-hop Action Network.
2007 Numerous hip-hop artists perform at the Live Earth concerts, which take place around the globe.

Sometimes it takes something big to make an individual change the path his life is taking. That was certainly true for The Game: five bullets showed him the direction he was going in. And he wasn't happy with what he saw.

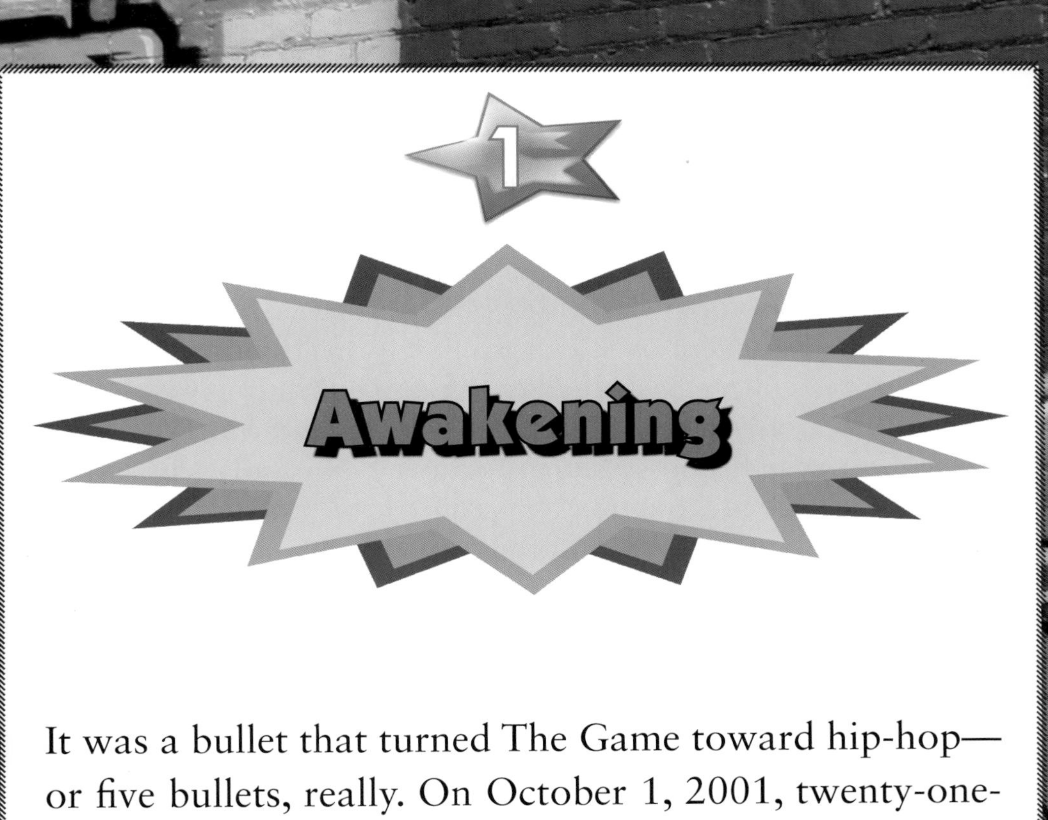

1 Awakening

It was a bullet that turned The Game toward hip-hop—or five bullets, really. On October 1, 2001, twenty-one-year-old Jayceon Taylor, sometimes called Game, was alone in his apartment in Bellflower, California, when he heard a knock on the door. Thinking the visitors were customers of the drug business he and his brother ran, he let them in. What happened next would change his life forever.

Three men, either burglars or rival gang members, entered the room. One attacked Jayceon and, as he tried to defend himself, another shot him five times. The intruders took all of the money and drugs in the apartment and left Jayceon for dead. Although bullets had struck his heart, stomach, leg, and arms, he miraculously remained conscious until the men left. Using his last bit of strength, he reached for his cell phone and called for help before slipping into a coma.

Street Life

A year before the shooting, Jayceon's considerable talent as a student and an athlete had earned him a basketball scholarship to Washington State University. He had grown up on the streets of Compton, just outside of Los Angeles, but it looked like those days were over. Unfortunately, his opportunity for a successful college basketball career and education was short lived. After only a few months at college, authorities found illegal drugs in his possession, took away his scholarship, and sent him back to Compton. Jayceon felt he was left with no legitimate opportunities, and embraced the "gangsta" lifestyle wholeheartedly.

Jayceon began selling drugs and stolen property to support himself. Unable to control him, his mother threw him out of her house. He and his older half-brother, Big Fase 100, moved into the projects of Bellflower, just outside of Compton, and began selling drugs from this new location. With characteristic commitment and dedication, Jayceon threw himself into his new business, and it wasn't long before he and Big Fase 100 were the most successful drug dealers in the area. But success in the ghetto created dangerous enemies, and it wasn't long before Jayceon found himself in a near-death situation, bleeding from five bullet wounds.

A Long Recovery

When Jayceon awoke two days after his shooting, he faced a long and difficult recovery. To help him through long, boring days in the hospital, Big Fase 100 brought him classic hip-hop albums to pass the time. As he slowly healed, Game absorbed the sounds of Notorious B.I.G., Snoop Dogg, Dr. Dre, Jay-Z, and the West Coast legends NWA. The angry, rebellious themes of ***oppression*** and crime in the music spoke to Jayceon. I could do this, he thought.

"How I Keep From Going Under"

For decades before Jayceon Taylor lay in his hospital bed thinking about his life, hip-hop artists had been rapping about their lives on the streets, about crime and poverty and injustice. Hip-hop was born in the 1970s in the poor neighborhoods of the Bronx in New York City, but young people all over the United States and other parts of the world soon adopted it as the ***culture*** and language that best expressed their feelings and experiences.

Rap music comes from a long line of musical ***genres*** expressing the black experience in America. Before slavery was

When one thinks of hip-hop, the first thing that probably comes to mind is music. But that's not the only way hip-hop culture is expressed. Graffiti artists turn walls into canvases for their work. To some, the results are works of art. To others, they are works of vandalism.

banned in 1865, slaves kept their African traditions and their sanity by singing songs together in rhythm while they worked. Gradually, African rhythms melded with European melodies to create blues music. Simultaneously, jazz began to take over the airwaves, giving a more complex voice to the black community. Then, in the words of blues master Muddy Waters, "the blues had a baby, and they called it rock n' roll." When rock n' roll went ***mainstream***, which meant "white" during the 1950s, black musicians turned to soul music and then funk to express themselves. The late 1970s saw the emergence of rap, with MCs like Grandmaster Flash and the Furious Five. Their first album, The Message, which came out in 1982, told the story of black oppression as it had never been told before. While previous musical genres had always expressed underly-

DJs were the kings in the early days of hip-hop. Their ability to cut, mix, and scratch albums on the turntables made some of them legends. Today, technology has taken over many of the skills that had made DJs stars.

ing themes of sorrow and oppression, Grandmaster Flash told his story with blatant honesty, angrily spitting lines like, "it's a jungle out here, sometimes I wonder how I keep from going under." This kind of direct truthfulness by Grandmaster Flash and others like him spoke to the many thousands of young black people who knew what he was talking about and had lived it every day.

Before MCs like Grandmaster Flash had begun rapping out raw, honest lyrics, though, DJs in poor Bronx neighborhoods had developed the music these words would go with. DJs like Kool Herc started setting up record turntables at block parties on the streets, switching between two turntables to keep the **break** going, extending the beat of a song to keep the dancers moving. This innovation of stripping a song down to its rhythm was the earliest form of hip-hop. The music of the DJs and the raps of the MCs came together to create a new genre called rap (sometimes also called hip-hop). Young people, first in the Bronx and then across the United States and around the world, got excited about the new sound. And while hip-hop grew up first in black neighborhoods, describing the experience of the black young people who lived there, before long people from many different cultures had begun creating their own forms of hip-hop.

A Final Decision

The rap artists who came before him inspired Jayceon to tell his own story. He also knew he had to find a legitimate way to support himself if he was to survive, and he made his choice: he'd become a hip-hop artist. He would use his experiences to tell the story of the streets.

In making this decision, Jayceon took on an enormous challenge. He had never even tried rapping before, so he would have to learn something entirely new. The odds were against him, but having a story to tell and a future to build, Jayceon was determined to become great.

Once Game made the decision to become a hip-hop star, he worked hard at it, perfecting the skills that would take him to the top. And it paid off—big time.

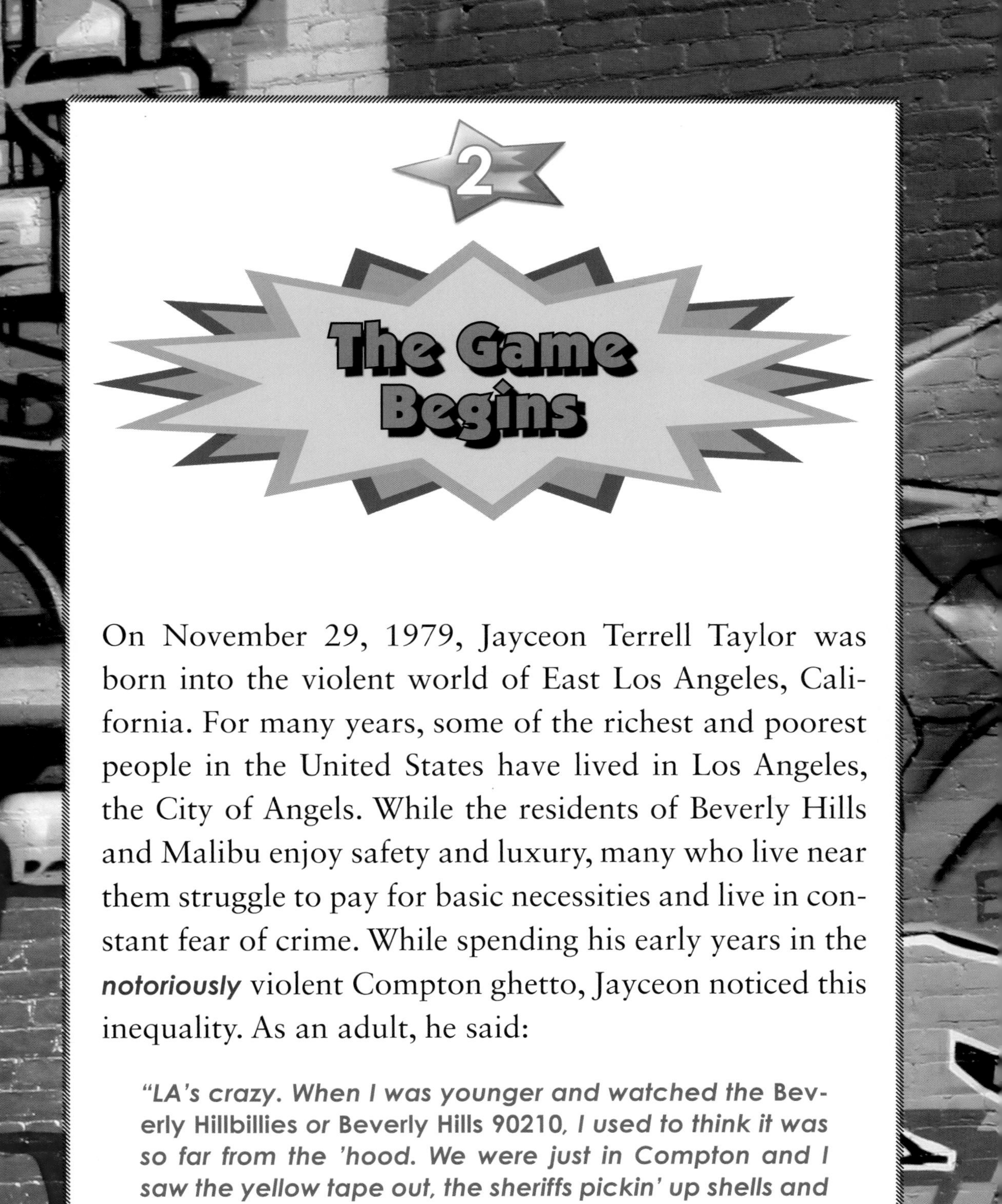

2

The Game Begins

On November 29, 1979, Jayceon Terrell Taylor was born into the violent world of East Los Angeles, California. For many years, some of the richest and poorest people in the United States have lived in Los Angeles, the City of Angels. While the residents of Beverly Hills and Malibu enjoy safety and luxury, many who live near them struggle to pay for basic necessities and live in constant fear of crime. While spending his early years in the ***notoriously*** violent Compton ghetto, Jayceon noticed this inequality. As an adult, he said:

> *"LA's crazy. When I was younger and watched the* Beverly Hillbillies *or* Beverly Hills 90210, *I used to think it was so far from the 'hood. We were just in Compton and I saw the yellow tape out, the sheriffs pickin' up shells and*

looking for someone to arrest and take to jail. We get on the freeway for 10 or 15 minutes, and we're in Beverly Hills, where we can sit in a Subway with no problems."

Although people lived a luxurious lifestyle right next door, the wealth seemed unreachable to Jayceon and his friends from Compton. He never dreamed he would one day be a part of it.

The Los Angeles area is one of great contrasts. The Game grew up in one of its poorest communities, an area filled with violence. Not far way, at least geographically, were shopping meccas like Beverly Hills's Rodeo Drive, shown here. To the people of Game's neighborhood, the shops might have well been on the other side of the planet.

Growing Up With Gangs

Growing up in Compton exposed Jayceon to the harsh reality of the ghetto at an early age. Life was often short and violent for those living in the poverty-stricken area, and many people joined gangs for protection, money, and a sense of community. Unfortunately, gang life often led to the destruction of those very things.

Jayceon's childhood memories reflect the violence that surrounded him. Both his mother, Lynette Baker, and his father, George Taylor, associated with gangs, and he remembers seeing them preparing to participate in a drive-by shooting. He also recalls a young neighbor being shot for nothing more than his clothes and shoes. But Jayceon would not let the constant presence of violence break his spirit. Instead, he later used these experiences to write the rap lyrics that would make him a star.

A Lonely Childhood

At seven years old, Jayceon experienced his first major loss. After one of his older sisters accused their father of sexual abuse, the State of California removed the Taylor children from their parents' home. While all of his brothers and sisters were placed with foster families, Jayceon spent most of his childhood in a kind of group home for boys in Carson, a town just west of Compton.

Although the home protected Jayceon from the violence of the ghetto, life was still not easy. Children of many different races lived in the group home, and the kids at school teased him for having Mexican and white brothers. He started lashing out with destructive behavior, and his elementary school nearly expelled him.

Despite the difficulties he endured, it was during these years that Jayceon began to show the skills that would ultimately make him successful. His caretakers often noticed him helping other children with their homework, and they commented on his natural intelligence. Jayceon even caught a glimpse of his bright future when he met a professional rapper for the first time. In 1989, he met Eazy-E, the gangsta rap pioneer and founder of revolutionary group NWA. "It was dope meeting Eazy," The Game said, years later "and it [made] a lasting impression." In fact, the rapper's influence became a major ingredient in Jayceon's success.

A Positive Influence

In spite of his difficult childhood, one person remained a constant source of inspiration and encouragement to Jayceon: his grandmother. When no one else thought Jayceon had a chance to make something of himself, she believed in him. In fact, she coined his stage name. When he was small, she noticed he was always "game" for anything, whether it was playing sports, riding bikes, or playing in the street, so she called him "The Game." She was so special to him that for many years he wore a tattoo of a butterfly on his cheek to remind him of her "life and how beautiful she was and the things she taught [him] before she passed." Game's only regret in life is that she died before she saw him fulfill his potential.

Tragedy Hits

At thirteen, Jayceon experienced a terrible loss that greatly affected his life. Things had been looking up for the Taylor family. Jayceon's brother Jevon was ***negotiating*** a record contract with MCA and looking forward to a bright future in music. Unfortunately, he wouldn't live to see his deal come through. One day, at a gas station, a rival shot Jevon in a fight over a girl.

When Jayceon visited his brother in the hospital, Jevon tearfully promised to make up for their time spent apart in foster care. He told Game, "I just want you to be good, 'cause

One way out of poverty was to become a sports star. Sure, it was a long shot, but others had succeeded, and there was reason to believe that Game would become one of those who used sports to get a better life. An incredibly bad choice ended Game's basketball career, though.

Mom and Dad is saying you [messin'] up." Later that day, at only seventeen years old, Jevon died. "I would rather him be alive and him rapping than me," The Game recently told *Rolling Stone* magazine, "I would give everything away if I could bring him back."

Caught Between Two Worlds

When Jayceon was fifteen, his mother regained custody of her children, and, with the exception of their father and Jevon, the Taylor family was reunited. Jayceon spent his later teenage years attending high school in Compton. Too full of hate and anger to follow his brother's advice to "be good," he rebelled and took his first steps toward gang life. Although the high school was Crips territory, Jayceon's older brother Big Fase 100 was a member of the Cedar Block Piru Bloods, and Jayceon followed in his footsteps.

Despite his dangerous gang ***affiliations***, Jayceon excelled at both school and sports. He played point guard for the high school's basketball team where he played alongside future NBA star Baron Davis. When it came time to apply for college, many universities offered Jayceon scholarships, and with them came the opportunity to escape the violent cycle of gang life. Graduating in 1999, Game chose Washington State University, and it looked as though was destined for success.

Back to the Streets

Just before Jayceon left for college, another of his brothers, Charles Bethea, lost his life to gang violence. With Jevon's death barely behind him, this new loss profoundly affected him. "People don't know what type of toll that takes on your life," he explains. "Especially being young and just fresh out in the world." Despite the opportunities presented to him, Jayceon could not turn away from gang life just yet.

When he was caught with drugs at college, Jayceon lost his basketball scholarship and left school before he'd completed even one semester. He went back to gang life, began dealing drugs, and ended up in the hospital. Game describes his brush with death as:

> ***"The biggest learning experience ever in my life. This sounds crazy, but I appreciate that happening to me because I'd probably be dead if it didn't. Anybody who gets shot and survives feels lucky. On the other hand I went through so much already that I felt somebody owed me. Now I could live out my dreams."***

Now, with a new goal in mind—becoming a rapper, Jayceon suddenly had something more than gangs and drugs to focus on. The real Game had begun.

The Game learned how to rhyme, and he learned how to rap. He took parts from East Coast rap and elements from rappers on the West Coast. In the end, though, he came up with his own style.

3

Building an Image

Jayceon had decided to become The Game, but before he could make the big time, he had a lot of work to do. He would have to learn how to rap before he could sell himself as an artist. But after everything he'd been through, Game was certain he could handle the challenge.

Learning His Craft

During his five-month recovery in the hospital after being shot, Game had plenty of time to learn his new craft. He knew that, like any artist who wants to develop his talent, he would have to study the masters, those artists who had created and defined the hip-hop movement. He listened to the CDs Big Fase 100 had given him over and over, carefully studying the songs and identifying the elements that made them great. He asked himself questions like, "How do successful rappers put words and ideas together to create a rhyming flow?" and "How do they put

The Game looked to the best when learning how to make the rhymes that would one day take him to the top of the hip-hop world. Among those who provided inspiration was Snoop Dogg.

together ***samples*** to create catchy melodies?" He explains part of his learning process:

> ***"I would jot down Jay-Z's rhymes, Snoop Dogg's rhymes, Ice Cube's rhymes, and kind of fix them so that they pertained a little bit more to me. And it went from that to me writing my own rhymes and it actually being my own story."***

East Coast, West Coast

Game studied two major styles of rap music while recovering: East Coast and West Coast. Each style had characteristics that made it unique. Originating in New York City, East Coast rap, like that of Notorious B.I.G. and Jay-Z, tended to be slower than West Coast. East Coast artists generally rapped complex vocal rhythms over sparse beats, creating a ***frenetic*** feel that mimicked the lifestyle of big cities like New York and Philadelphia. East Coast rap addressed a variety of subjects, including politics, life on the streets, and personal relationships.

West Coast rap, generally associated with Los Angeles, had an easier, more rhythmic feel. Although the beats tended to be faster, West Coast rappers used simpler rhythmic patterns, re-creating sunny California's laid-back feel. Snoop Dogg and Dr. Dre ***epitomized*** West Coast rap. Los Angeles was also the gang capital of the United States, and West Coast hip-hop often addressed the subject of criminal life in the area.

A Style of His Own

After immersing himself in rap from both coasts, The Game formed his own style. Relying heavily on the West Coast style, like a faster beat and simple rhythmic patterns in his lyrics, Game created a new, fresh sound by adding some East Coast elements. He would often break up his laid-back flow with more complex rhythms, and his intense, angry delivery paid tribute to East Coast artists. The Game wrote lyrics that were more story-oriented than many other rappers in the West Coast gangsta rap genre. Although his subject matter reflected his life as a criminal, his raps also discussed other subjects, like becoming a father. "I mixed everybody's style into one," he says. "That's why some people feel that I sound like I'm from the East Coast, even though I rap about the West Coast."

Black Wall Street

At first, Game's rhymes were weak, but after many months of practice, his flow improved and he felt ready to show off his new skills. Now he needed an audience. He decided the best way to gain exposure was to start his own record company.

He and Big Fase 100 wanted a name for their project that would reflect their pride in the black community. After doing some research, they settled on Black Wall Street Records. During the Oklahoma oil boom of the 1910s, a wealthy black residential district sprouted up in Tulsa, Oklahoma, and people dubbed it "the Black Wall Street." Unfortunately, some people were angry about the presence of the successful black community, and burned down much of the area in the 1921 Race Riot. Within five years of the riot, the residents had pooled their resources and rebuilt much of their community. The Game and Big Fase 100 wanted to carry on the spirit of persistence and courage demonstrated by the residents of Black Wall Street.

Before Black Wall Street Records could begin making a profit, Game and Big Fase 100 needed to record and promote their artists. First, Big Fase 100 and Game recorded a ***mixtape*** of The Game's songs and began circulating it in ***underground*** rap circles. They also began to record and promote other artists like Glasses Malone, Vita, and Nu Jerzey Devil.

Underground Rap vs. Mainstream Rap

In forming a record company, Game and Big Fase 100 had entered the underground hip-hop scene. The music industry consisted of two levels, underground and mainstream. To be a part of the hip-hop underground, an artist needed only a desire to create rap and basic recording equipment. Once he had these two things, he could record a mixtape of his songs. A mixtape was a recording of one or more artists. It could be either longer, shorter, or the same length as a regular album—the only difference was the production quality, in other words, how an album sounded. An album with low production quality was usually recorded on simple, cheap equipment in either a small or home studio, typically with little-known musicians. Because of the quality of the equipment, the recording often sounded slightly fuzzy and sometimes had a few mistakes. If the musicians were good, though, the recording could have a raw sound that many people liked. After an artist recorded a mixtape, he or she could distribute it to get publicity before starting to perform in underground **venues**. These performances often took place in small clubs, warehouses, or even people's homes. Participating in the underground scene helped artists gain an audience and create a buzz about their sound.

The mainstream scene, on the other hand, consisted of a few well-known artists and producers. Generally, the artists seen on TV and in magazines like *Source* and *Vibe* were mainstream artists. Their albums were recorded in large studios on complex, expensive equipment that the average budding musician could only dream about. They used highly paid, professional musicians, and their albums generally had a better sound that was clearer than underground albums. Because these artists

Whether mainstream or underground, the purpose of rap music was the same—get the crowd up on its feet and dancing.

appeared on TV, they had a much larger audience than underground artists and therefore could play in large venues around the world. Although artists could become popular and make a living in the underground, the only way to become extremely rich and reach "star" status was through the mainstream. The Game was determined to be a star, but first he would have to prove himself to the hardcore underground rap fans.

First Record Deal

The Game released his first mixtape, *You Know What It Is Vol. 1*, in 2002, and received his first bit of recognition when he attended a hip-hop summit hosted by Russell Simmons and Louis Farrakhan. At the summit, rappers, both known and unknown, gathered to perform, and people shared information on hip-hop-related products and issues. Shortly after the summit, The Game gained the attention of JT the Bigga Figga, CEO of the independent label Get Low Recordz, who offered him a record deal. Although a company usually signs an artist for a certain number of albums on the condition that the artist will not record with anyone else, JT gave Game a rare opportunity; Get Low Recordz signed The Game for a short three-album record deal that did not require him to work exclusively with their label. JT explains his decision to give The Game this freedom in a 2005 interview, explaining that he, "was teaching [Game] how to do the independent thing, and that's why [he] didn't sign him as an artist." In other words, JT wanted Game to learn how to support himself in the underground rap scene, so he didn't want to tie him down. In the next few months, Game would be offered a very unexpected opportunity that would lead out of the underground scene and into the mainstream in one of the fastest climbs to stardom in rap history.

One of the biggest names in hip-hop is Dr. Dre. He's a performer, a producer, and a business mogul. Dr. Dre has also played an important role in helping other musicians reach their peak. Among them is The Game.

A Chance at the Big Time

While Game worked on his first two albums with JT, his mix-tape continued to circulate, and mainstream record companies began to take interest in The Game. Sean "P. Diddy" Combs was the first major label producer to hear Game's music, and they began negotiating a contract. But before Combs could close the deal, Game received the opportunity of a lifetime.

Game had always idolized legendary rap group NWA. "Everything about a father throwing a baseball to his son in the suburbs, that's what NWA was to me. They were the only role models I had besides Michael Jordan." Now one of their members, rapper-turned-producer-turned-music mogul Dr. Dre, wanted to make Game his **protégé** and sign him to his label, Aftermath Entertainment. The decision was obvious for Game. He abandoned the deal with P. Diddy and signed with Aftermath. Later, The Game described his first meeting with Dr. Dre, saying that:

> ***"The best moment I've had in rap was walking into his studio in 2002 and Dre saying he heard a mix tape of my freestyles and wanted to sign me. Trying to act cool? I was frozen. I'm still star struck with Dre."***

Playing the Fields

The Game's decision to abandon the underground scene was controversial. Many die-hard rap fans saw the move toward the mainstream as selling out. But Game didn't leave the underground scene right away; in fact, he remained a large part of it for the next two years. While working with Dr. Dre on his first major label recording, The Game released his first album, Untold Story, on Get Low Recordz. The album, which featured artists like Sean T., Young Noble (of the Outlawz), and JT the Bigga Figga, sold 82,000 records within three months.

People who wouldn't normally have listened to hip-hop became familiar with some of the big names—like Kanye West, Ludacris, and the Game—when Boost Mobile used them in their commercials.

The Game knew it was important to build a solid fan base, so he spent his time networking and gaining exposure. If there was already a lot of buzz about him in the underground, his new record would sell more copies. He appeared on mixtapes hosted by DJ Kayslay, DJ Whoo Kid, and DJ Clue, among others, and sharpened his performance skills playing small rap shows. In order to solidify his connections with major label players, he appeared on the underground single "Certified Gangsta" with Juelz Santana and Jim Jones. He also released his second mixtape, *You Know What It Is Vol. 2*, and his own single, "Westside Story," on Black Wall Street Records. He could also be heard on the song "Can't Stop Me" by Fredwreck on the video game *NBA Live 2004*.

In addition to working on the underground rap scene, Game popularized his image by appearing in P. Diddy's Sean John clothing ads and Boost mobile commercials with Kanye West and Ludacris. By the end of that year, Game had positioned himself well. He was ready to go mainstream and become a rap star.

Under Dr. Dre's guidance, The Game learned how to put out a successful recording. The process was much longer than he liked, but Dr. Dre proved that the added effort was worth it. Before long, The Game was racking up one success after another.

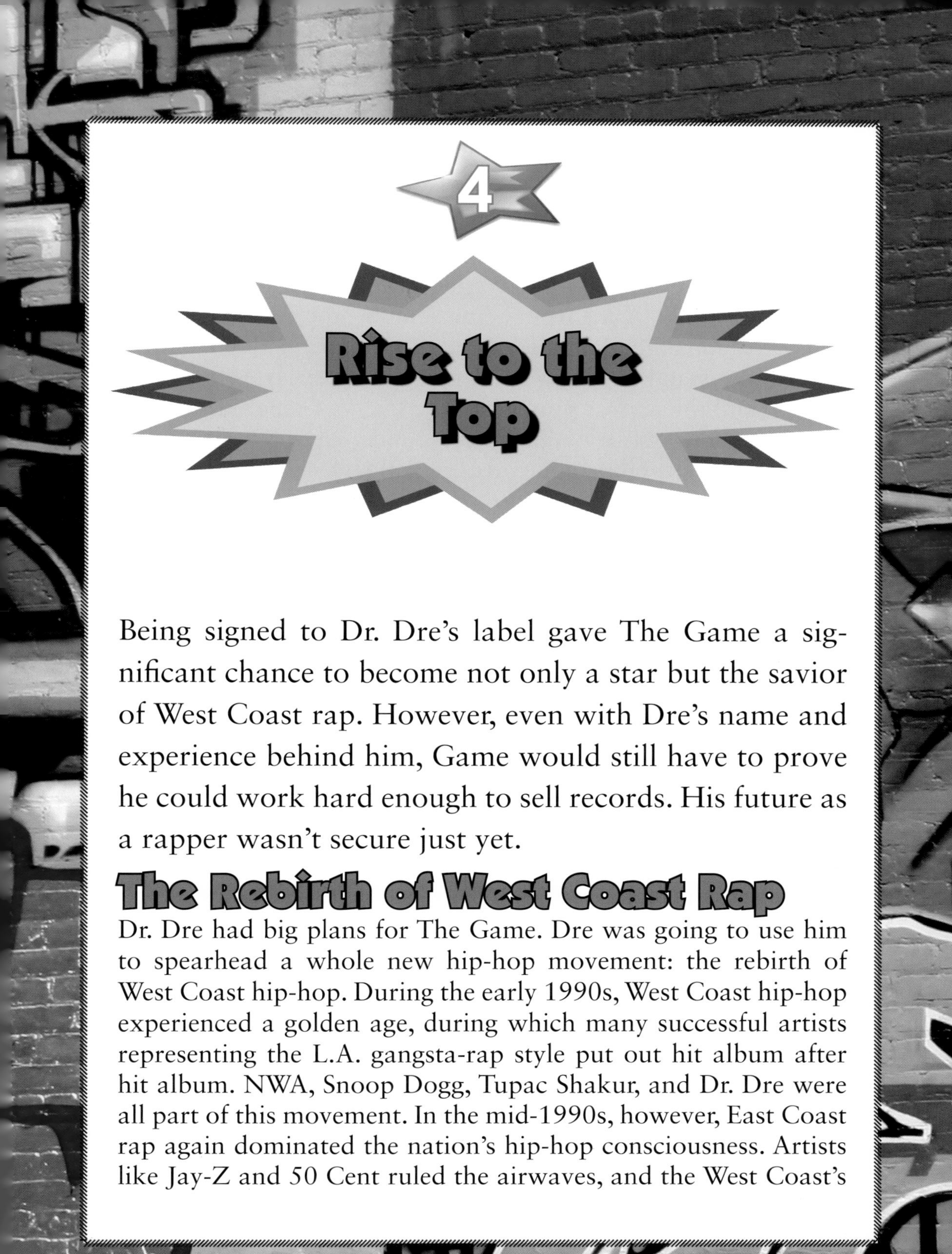

4

Rise to the Top

Being signed to Dr. Dre's label gave The Game a significant chance to become not only a star but the savior of West Coast rap. However, even with Dre's name and experience behind him, Game would still have to prove he could work hard enough to sell records. His future as a rapper wasn't secure just yet.

The Rebirth of West Coast Rap

Dr. Dre had big plans for The Game. Dre was going to use him to spearhead a whole new hip-hop movement: the rebirth of West Coast hip-hop. During the early 1990s, West Coast hip-hop experienced a golden age, during which many successful artists representing the L.A. gangsta-rap style put out hit album after hit album. NWA, Snoop Dogg, Tupac Shakur, and Dr. Dre were all part of this movement. In the mid-1990s, however, East Coast rap again dominated the nation's hip-hop consciousness. Artists like Jay-Z and 50 Cent ruled the airwaves, and the West Coast's influence decreased. Los Angeles had failed to produce a major rap star for too long, and Dr. Dre was determined to put an end to the streak of East Coast domination.

To do this, Dre knew he needed a rapper who not only rapped about the West Coast gangsta lifestyle, but who had actually lived it. Aside from being genuine, the rapper needed to have something unique about his image, something to make him stand out from the rappers of the early 1990s. Dr. Dre found the perfect protégé in The Game. Game's troubled history, along with his gunshot wounds, gave him undeniable street credibility, while his original style and message of redemption gave him a fresh new edge. Dre had found the perfect rapper to lead his new movement.

Recording the First Album

Dre had gained experience as a successful teacher when he produced Snoop Dogg years earlier, and he took The Game under his wing in just the same way he had Snoop. Dre taught his new protégé the secrets of working in a studio, as well as the musical concepts he would need to know in order to be an effective recording artist, like counting musical ***bars***. This skill helped an artist pick up where he left off if a recording was interrupted.

Reported clashes occurred between Dr. Dre and The Game during this period. Game, an eager student, was anxious to finish his first major label debut quickly, while Dre wanted to take his time and make sure each track was perfect. Despite their differences, Game and Dre forged a strong personal relationship. Aside from teaching The Game the practical aspects of the hip-hop industry, Dre also became Game's spiritual mentor. Game describes Dre as "the father I never had."

Dre wanted The Game's first album to be huge, and he did everything he could to make it the most successful hip-hop album possible. He had an ear for the qualities necessary for singles and superior sampling skills, both of which he used to create several songs that would be both original and ***marketable***. Dre recruited other famous hip-hop producers, such as Kanye West and Timbaland, to produce several of the tracks, giving the album variety and heightened marketability. He also used guest artists such as Mary J. Blige, 50 Cent, Busta Rhymes, and Eminem, which accomplished the same thing. When the album, to be called *The Documentary*, had finally been ***mastered*** and was ready to be released, Dre had created a certain hit.

The Newest Member of G-Unit

To ensure the biggest success for The Game's first album, Dre wanted to create a buzz around his new artist. Since the West Coast had been off the mainstream hip-hop radar for so long, he knew collaboration with East Coast artists would generate hype. Dre made an agreement with Jimmy Iovine, chairman of Interscope Records, to have Game become a part of G-Unit, the successful East Coast rap crew led by 50 Cent that included rappers Lloyd Banks, Young Buck, and Tony Yayo. The pairing was meant to give The Game instant credibility, while at the same time drawing more attention to G-Unit. Game soon began appearing in music videos by 50 Cent, Lloyd Banks, and Young Buck. In return, Game featured G-Unit rappers on several tracks on *The Documentary*.

"A Soldier Is Born"

On June 30, 2003, while still in the process of recording *The Documentary*, Game's first long-term girlfriend, Aleska, gave birth to his first son, Harlem Caron Taylor. Game said later that watching the birth of his son was the best moment of his life. The experience brought him to the "next level—I've never been so happy. I wanted to bring him into the world so much that I was going, 'Come on!'"

As a tribute to his new child, The Game wrote the song "Like Father, Like Son," in which he describes the details of

Harlem's birth and gives him advice about the future. In the chorus he tells him, "But in the end I hope you only turn out better than me, I hope you know I love you young'un, like father, like son." The Game wrote later that his dream for Harlem was to see him graduate college.

The Documentary Breaks

By New Year's Day of 2005, when recording on *The Documentary* finished, The Game had released one underground album, appeared in numerous hip-hop videos, sharpened his performance skills on the mixtape circuit, and popularized his image by appearing in mainstream ads and video games. He had done everything he could to ensure the success of his first album, and it was about to pay off. Aftermath records released *The Documentary* on January 18, 2005. Within one week, the album had sold 586,000 copies and was #1 on the *Billboard* charts. Of the best-selling albums of 2005, *The Documentary* took tenth place. In the United Kingdom, the album debuted at #7, and it sold over 5 million copies around the world. The album had two hit singles, "How We Do" and "Hate It or Love It." When "Hate It or Love It" earned two Grammy nominations, the chorus of this autobiographical song must have described how The Game felt: "Hate it or love it, underdog's on top, and I'm gonna shout, homie, until my heart stop."

A Constant Presence in the Underground

Several months after *The Documentary* came out, JT the Bigga Figga released *West Coast Resurrection* and *Untold Story Volume 2 (Chopped and Screwed)*, two albums Game had recorded with him before he met Dre. Although these albums did not receive critical acclaim, they sold well by independent standards, due to the success of *The Documentary*.

West Coast Resurrection sold 1,000 copies in New York, an unusually high number for an album by a West Coast artist, and Game said he was, "glad to hear his mixtape be heard in the birthplace of hip-hop." Meanwhile, Game put out two more mixtapes, *You Know What It Is Vol. 3* and *Ghost Unit*, on his own record label, Black Wall Street Records.

Feuds

On the streets, you must earn and keep the respect of your peers. Competition can often turn deadly, and getting the upper hand is a matter of survival. Although successful rappers no longer need to embrace street mentality to provide for themselves, they often keep alive the spirit of violent competition in their songs and lifestyles. Rap feuds, in which rappers publicly insult each other in songs, magazines, and on the radio, are a big part of the hip-hop world. Although public feuding can lead to violence, it benefits the rappers by creating hype around them. Fans take sides and follow the feuds of their favorite rappers like audio soap operas. Game explains that although rappers appear to be angry with each other:

> ***"They don't really care man. At the end of the day they gon' say [they hate me] but controversy, beef—all that [stuff]—is what sells hip hop; it's what sells anything in the world. . . . I think that hip-hop beef is healthy as long as it doesn't tear away from the big picture or become violent or tragic as it did with Tupac and Biggie."***

The Game became involved in several rap feuds, the most famous of which was his feud with 50 Cent. From the beginning of their relationship, tension brewed between them. 50 Cent felt that since The Game was now a member of his G-Unit crew, he should openly take his side in all of his many feuds. The Game refused, going so far as to say he would like to work with some of 50 Cent's enemies, such as Nas and Jadakiss. After the release of *The Documentary*, 50 Cent claimed he had helped write six of the songs and that Game wasn't giving him enough credit for his success. The Game denied this, and dismissed 50 Cent's anger as jealousy. After all, 50 Cent's new album had been pushed back as a result of *The Documentary*'s success. It would only be a matter of time before their feud came to a dangerous head.

When The Game became part of 50 Cent's G-Unit, it helped create the buzz that can make or break an album. It also brought G-Unit to the attention of a new group of fans. Unfortunately, it also led to a feud between The Game and 50 Cent.

A False Ending

On February 28, 2005, The Game and his ***entourage*** confronted 50 Cent outside the Hot 97 radio station in New York. According to witnesses, they exchanged angry words and, after a confrontation, one of Game's entourage was shot in the leg. No one was sure who pulled the trigger.

Concerned by this incident, as well as other feuds taking place between his clients, Jimmy Iovine of Interscope records arranged a peace meeting in which many hip-hop artists would reconcile their rivalries. The Game and 50 Cent shook hands, announced the end of their rivalry, and donated over 200,000 dollars each to inner-city charities in their respective hometowns of Compton and Harlem. But many fans saw the move as a publicity stunt and weren't surprised at what happened next.

Despite their supposed reconciliation, 50 Cent continued to insult Game, telling the media that The Game's street credibility was a lie. In retaliation, Game launched a boycott of 50 Cent and G-Unit, called G-Unot, and released a "diss" song insulting 50 Cent in his new mixtape *You Know What It Is Vol. 3*. 50 Cent responded by portraying Game as a Mr. Potato Head doll in one of his videos. He also told *XXL*, a popular hip-hop magazine, that The Game's next album was sure to fail without him. Game was determined to prove him wrong.

The Game's feud with 50 Cent led to his not-so-friendly departure from G-Unit. Now he sought out the best in the business to help him with his next album, including producer Scott Storch.

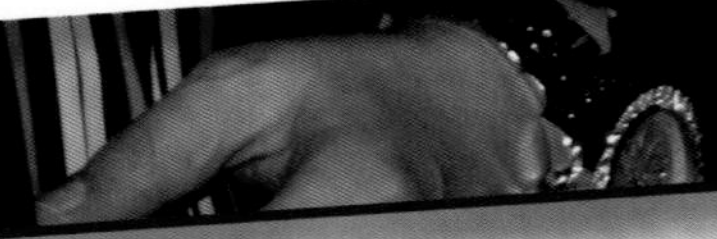

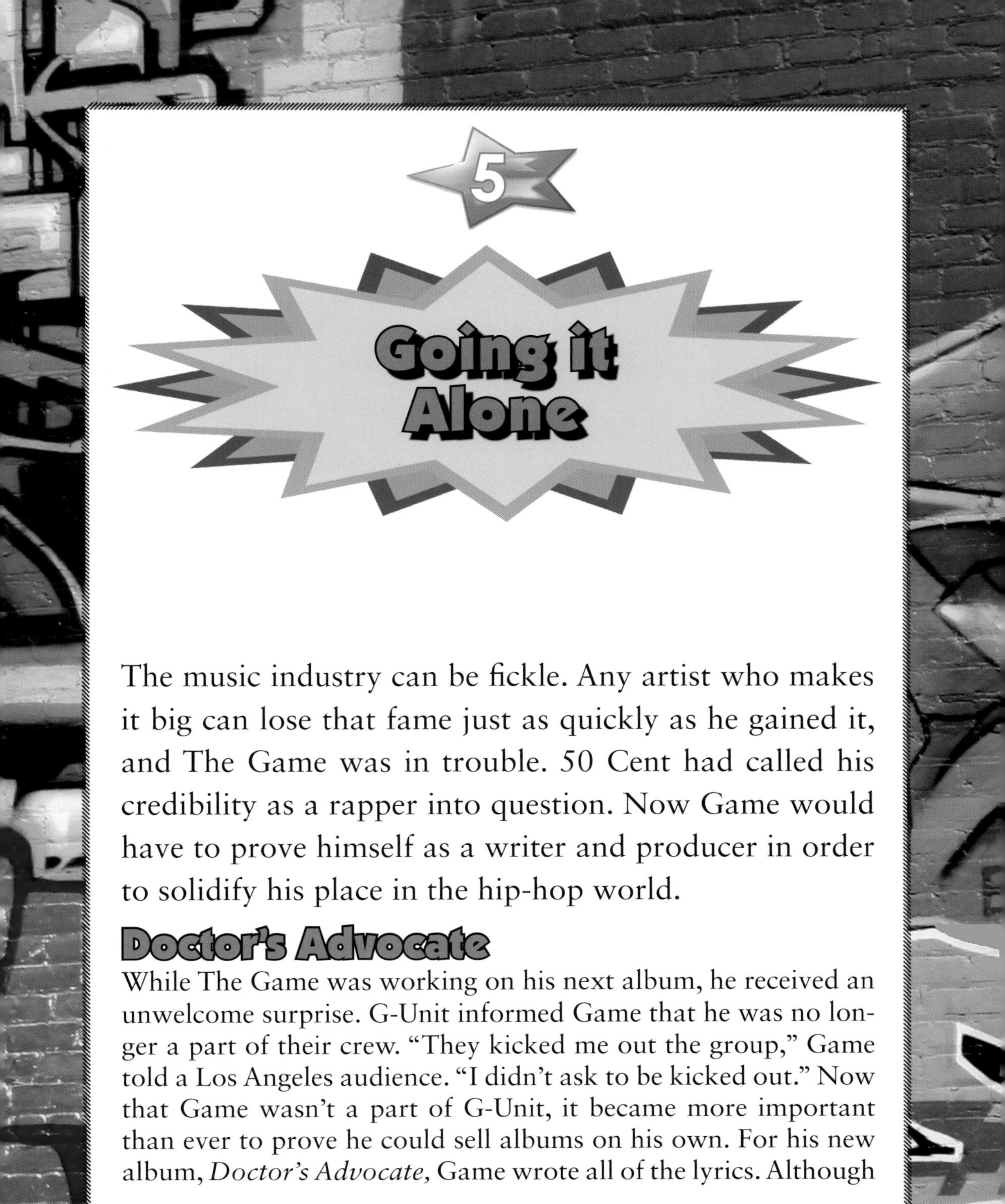

5

Going it Alone

The music industry can be fickle. Any artist who makes it big can lose that fame just as quickly as he gained it, and The Game was in trouble. 50 Cent had called his credibility as a rapper into question. Now Game would have to prove himself as a writer and producer in order to solidify his place in the hip-hop world.

Doctor's Advocate

While The Game was working on his next album, he received an unwelcome surprise. G-Unit informed Game that he was no longer a part of their crew. "They kicked me out the group," Game told a Los Angeles audience. "I didn't ask to be kicked out." Now that Game wasn't a part of G-Unit, it became more important than ever to prove he could sell albums on his own. For his new album, *Doctor's Advocate,* Game wrote all of the lyrics. Although

Dr. Dre didn't produce any of the tracks, Game refers to him not only on the album's cover, but also throughout the record. When asked why he decided on the title he said, "Dr. Dre's the man; what he says goes." But the name is more than just an **homage** to his mentor. Game talked about the other meanings of the title in a later interview:

> ***"I feel like Hip Hop needs surgery. Nas say Hip Hop is dead. I don't say Hip Hop is dead, I just say Hip Hop is down, so on this album I'm the doctor. And the advocate—you gotta know the definition of advocate: to advocate for someone, some place or something. But I'm advocating for a lot of people on this one: for my hometown, Compton; for Hip Hop; for the whole Hip Hop generation—from the west to everybody. That's the definition behind the title."***

Recording the Second Album

Unwilling to take any chances on his second album, Game recruited the best in the business to produce several of its tracks. Kanye West produced the melodic single "You Wouldn't Get Far," in which Game warns women not to use their looks to gain status, and Scott Storch produced the jazz- and funk-influenced "Let's Ride," among others. In addition to these two singles, *Doctor's Advocate* featured "It's Ok (One Blood)," on which Game collaborates with **reggae** artist Junior Reid, and "Why You Hate the Game" with Marcia Ambrosius from Floetry. The Game also featured some of the up-and-coming artists from Black Wall Street Records, giving them the chance to experience the spotlight.

The Southern Influence

Until recently, East Coast and West Coast were the only major styles of hip-hop. However, since 2002, Southern rap has been on the rise. Southern style rap, or "Dirty South" rap, is either very slow or very fast and characterized by simple beats; a laid-back, rhythmic delivery; and melodic samples.

Usually in order to have a successful second album, an artist needs to expand on their style. The Game updated his music by incorporating these elements of Southern rap into several tracks on *Doctor's Advocate*. In contrast to the intense, East Coast–style rapping he had used on *The Documentary*, Game's rhymes were more relaxed, and he slowed down his delivery.

When The Game was ready to cut his second album, he called on the best in the business to ensure its success. One of those was Kanye West. Though now perhaps best known as a singer, Kanye also has a reputation as an extremely successful producer.

Fans loved The Game on his own. To prove it, they snapped up his music as soon as it became available. The success of his second album proved that 50 Cent was wrong. The Game could sell records quite nicely without him, thank you very much!

You can hear the Dirty South influence on "You Crazy," and "You Wouldn't Get Far."

Breaking the Album Alone

After months of recording in the studio, The Game had an album with a hip new sound and several strong singles. Having created the album without help from Dre or G-Unit, Game set out to prove that not only could he make a record independently, but he could sell it too. On August 1, 2006, just a few months before the release of *Doctor's Advocate*, The Game officially announced he had parted ways with Aftermath Records and signed with Geffen. The album's release would test 50 Cent's claim that Game couldn't sell records without him.

Doctor's Advocate hit store shelves on November 14, 2006, and sold 358,988 copies in its first week, hitting #1 on the *Billboard* 200 and charting around the world. The album's success meant that Jayceon Taylor had finally proven he could truly play the game.

"One More Gone"

The verdict was clear: the public loved The Game. Not only were his album sales fantastic, but in an unscientific poll of 1,280 rap fans taken by About.com, 44 percent said The Game was their favorite rapper. The Game had succeeded in reviving West Coast rap and making a name for himself.

Despite his success, Game claims his next album will be his last:

> *"I think three classic albums are good for me, you know, I got my point across . . . I was a prominent figure on the West Coast . . . [and] hip-hop as a whole. I think I made my impact . . . enough for my name to be . . . remembered. That's it for me—one more gone."*

The Game is more than a music icon. He's a father, he is involved in films, and perhaps most important, he is involved in charity events. This helps to keep The Game grounded in reality.

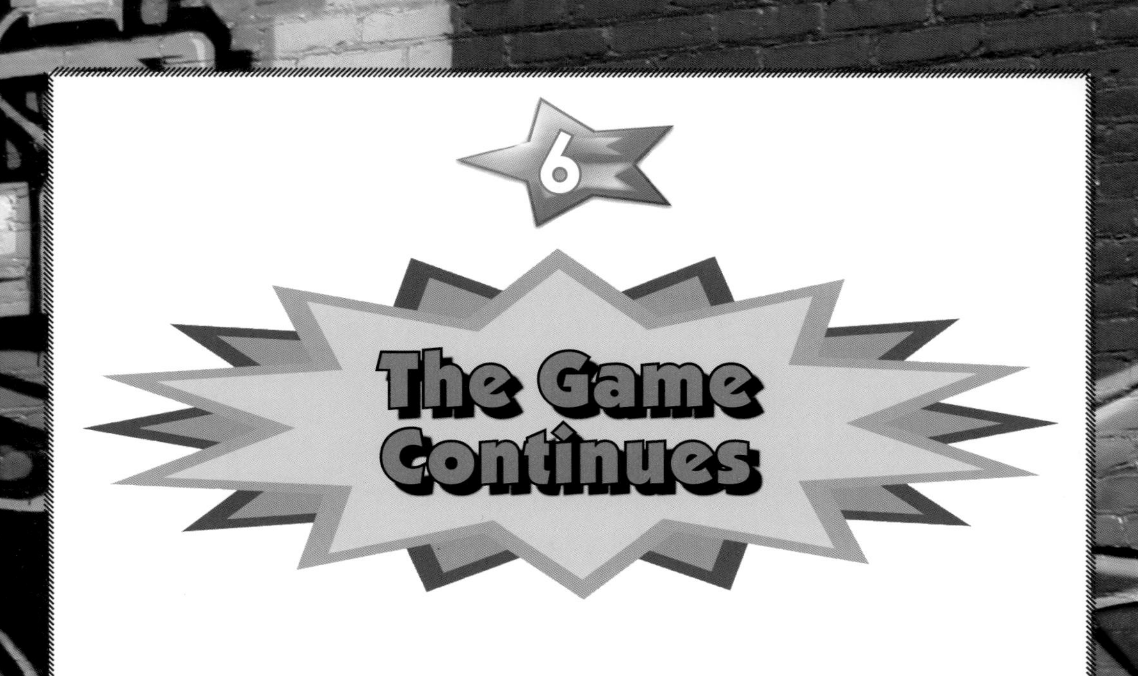

6 The Game Continues

The Game may have fulfilled his dream of becoming a rap star, but his career is far from over. Whether with romance, fatherhood, acting, or charity work, The Game will always be a very busy man.

Love

Since becoming famous, The Game has had a rocky love life. In his song "Dreams" on *The Documentary*, he expressed his wish to date R&B star Mya. His dream came true shortly after the record broke, and the two dated briefly. Later he was linked to Irish pop star Samantha Mumba. In 2006, he proposed to model and actress Valeisha Butterfield, the daughter of North Carolina congressman G. K. Butterfield, but their engagement was short lived, and The Game began dating former substitute teacher Tiffany Webb. In an interview with *Complex* magazine,

Game explained why he prefers dating regular women to celebrities:

> *"[Dating celebrities] is cool, but [it] has got its ups and downs. The up is you kinda feel hot, the Jay-Z and Beyoncé thing. The downside is that you don't get to spend as much time with double celebrity [work]. Then there's the thing that they be switching up—you take my girlfriend now, I'll take your boyfriend . . . so I'm pretty much done at this point. I'll keep a regular [girlfriend]."*

Fatherhood

The Game says that he loves being a father. He takes his four-year-old, Harlem, with him to Europe because he "can't go three weeks without seeing him." Game wants Harlem to be involved in the entertainment business, and he already has deals pending with Sean John and possibly Huggies. On April 25, 2007, The Game's girlfriend, Tiffany Webb, gave birth to his second son, King Justice Taylor. When asked if he could give one trait to his children, Game answered:

> *"Loyalty. Loyalty will take you a long way in life. Even if you're just living a semi-wealthy, all-American life. It'll get you the two-story house with the minivan, the white picket fence, the dog, the wife, and the kids. If you're loyal to your parents, your teachers, your friends, your mate, your kids, your job, nobody could say you're a bad guy."*

Movies and DVDs

In addition to music, The Game is also involved in the film industry. Starting out with a self-titled documentary of his own life in 2005, Game now has six films under his belt, including *Infamous Times: The Original 50 Cent* and *Tournament of Dreams*. He is best known as an actor for his portrayal of Big Meat in *Waist Deep*, a gangsta drama in which he played the villain. In 2006, he released the DVD/documentary *The Game: Stop Snitchin, Stop Lyin*, about his experiences in the rap industry, together with a mixtape of the same name. The Game also stars in *Millionaire Boyz Club*, set to be released in

The Game's oldest son, Harlem, often travels with him. And Harlem has an entertainment career on the horizon as well. The Game takes his role as a father very seriously.

When Hurricane Katrina hit the Gulf Coast of the United States, it left many communities and lives in ruins. The Game participated in many relief efforts, even donating a portion of the proceeds from the sale of the sneakers he designed as part of his shoe line.

2007, a movie about a young man coming back to the streets after getting out of prison.

Charity Work

Inspired by the philanthropy of Eazy-E, The Game feels it is his duty to give back to his community. Shortly after he hit celebrity status, he partnered with 310 Motoring, a car-customizing company, to put out his own line of shoes. In August of 2005, The Game was developing the sneaker, called "The Hurricane," when Hurricane Katrina struck the Gulf Coast on August 29, destroying much of New Orleans and leaving more than 1,800 dead and hundreds of thousands more homeless. Rather than rename his shoe, The Game decided to donate a portion of the proceeds to help rebuild New Orleans. When asked how long this will continue, he answered, "until the company ceases to exist or until New Orleans is 100% rebuilt." The Game also auctioned off a brand new, tricked-out Bentley given to him by 310 Motoring and donated all of the proceeds to Katrina victims.

Although Hurricane Katrina is a major concern of Game's, he also gives to projects that help poor communities. At Game's unsuccessful reconciliation with 50 Cent in 2005, he donated money to the struggling Boys' Choir of Harlem. Founded in 1968, the choir also had a school, The Choir Academy of Harlem, which was in desperate need of funds. The Game and 50 Cent were some of the first to answer their call for help. At the same event, Game also donated money to the Compton Unified School District's music program, in order to give back to the community that raised him.

The Game on Gang Violence

Many critics accuse gangsta rap of glorifying violence. They feel the lyrics influence young men and women living in poverty to participate in an unhealthy lifestyle that increases their chances of ending up dead or in jail. When asked about whether his album encourages participation in gang life, Game stated:

> ***"I'm telling my story. I'm out to please no one but my-self. I'm not telling anybody to sell drugs or pick up guns. When I sold drugs it was because it was my last resort, because I had four sisters and an older brother and we were eating Cheerios on Thanksgiving. When I picked up a gun it was because my life was threat-ened. . . . I'm not glorifying the life I lived because I wouldn't wish that on anybody—I'm just one human being raised in the 'hood who wanted nothing more than to get out."***

Black Wall Street

While many stars leave their communities and never look back, The Game continues to visit his old neighborhood in Compton, where the Black Wall Street headquarters is located. "I'm not a star," he insists, "I'm just a regular guy who has a great rap album." He still owns multiple properties in the area, and despite the constant threat of violence calls it his "comfort zone."

When he's not touring or recording, Game works to build up the Black Wall Street. Although it started out as a record company, BWS has grown into a multifaceted business as well as a nonprofit organization. The company's mission is "The Rebirth and Renaissance of Urban America and Abroad." As of 2007, Black Wall Street consisted of four branches: fashion (apparel), music (record label), community development (real estate investment), and gang intervention (nonprofit organization). The company also wants to publish books, the first being a biography of Game's brother, Big Fase 100. The Game explained the mentality at the heart of BWS:

"People think it's just a record label, but it's a lot bigger than that . . . Black Wall Street stands for all the black lives America couldn't kill . . . We the black people man. It ain't about Blood or Crip . . . it's about unity. That's something that we done lacked in the L.A. area man for a long time. . . . We gotta reconcile."

A Last Word

On his private MySpace site, Game sums up his story:

"I came from nothing. Turned nothing into something and something into what I am today. A great father, the son of a proud mother, a wise man, a blessed individual, a gangsta and a gentlemen groomed into one of hip-hop's elite M.C.s!!!"

But, he adds, "I am no better than anyone else."

1970s Hip-hop is born in the Bronx, New York.

Nov. 29, 1970 Jayceon Terrell Taylor—The Game—is born in East Los Angeles, California.

1989 The Game meets Eazy-E, pioneer of gangsta rap.

1990s Gangsta rap is hot on the West Coast.

1999 Game graduates from high school.

Oct. 1, 2001 The Game is shot five times.

2002 The Game releases his first mixtape.

Game works with hip-hop legend Dr. Dre.

Dirty South makes the rap scene.

2003 Game becomes a father for the first time.

2004 Game's first album is released.

2005 Two additional albums are released independently.

Game donates a portion of the sales of his sneaker line to hurricane relief efforts.

Game donates money to the Boys' Choir of Harlem.

Police officers in North Carolina disclose that they are suing The Game for defamation, based on the aftermath of Game's arrest following an incident at a shopping mall.

Jan. 2005 *The Documentary* is released.

Feb. 2005 The Game and his entourage are involved in a shooting with 50 Cent.

Nov. 2006 *Doctor's Advocate* is released.

2007 The Game becomes a father again with the birth of his second son.

He stars in *Millionaire Boyz Club*.

The Game is arrested on charges of threatening another person.

Albums

Studio

2005 *The Documentary*

2006 *Doctor's Advocate*

Independent Releases

2004 *Untold Story*

2005 *Untold Story (Chopped and Screwed)*

2005 *Untold Story, Vol. 2*

2005 *West Coast Resurrection*

2006 *G.A.M.E.*

Number-One Single

2005 "Hate It or Love It" (with 50 Cent)

DVDs

2005 *The Documentary*

2006 *Doctor's Advocate*

2006 *The Game: Stop Snitchin, Stop Lyin*

2005 *Beef 3*

2005 *Infamous Times: The Original 50 Cent*

2004 *Life in a Day: The DVD*

Films

2006 *Waist Deep*

2007 *Tournament of Dreams*

2007 *Millionaire Boyz Club*

Books

Bogdanov, Vladimir, Chris Woodstra, Steven Thomas Erlewine, and John Bush (eds.). *All Music Guide to Hip-Hop: The Definitive Guide to Rap and Hip-Hop*. San Francisco, Calif.: Backbeat Books, 2003.

Chang, Jeff. Can't Stop Won't Stop: A History of the Hip-Hop Generation. New York: Picador, 2005.

George, Nelson. *Hip Hop America*. New York: Penguin, 2005.

Kusek, Dave, and Gerd Leonhard. *The Future of Music: Manifesto for the Digital Music Revolution*. Boston, Mass.: Berkley Press, 2005.

Light, Alan (ed.). *The Vibe History of Hip Hop*. New York: Three Rivers Press, 1999.

Waters, Rosa. *Hip-Hop: A Short History*. Broomall, Pa.: Mason Crest, 2007.

Watkins, S. Craig. *Hip Hop Matters: Politics, Pop Culture, and the Struggle for the Soul of a Movement*. Boston, Mass.: Beacon Press, 2006.

Web Sites

Black Wall Street Records
www.therealblackwallstreet.com

The Game
www.comptongame.com

The Game on My Space
www.myspace.com/thegame

The Game 360
web.thegame360.com

Glossary

affiliations—Groups with close connections.

bars—A basic unit of time in music, based on the number of beats.

break—The part in a rap song in which only the beat is heard, no vocals or other instruments.

culture—The shared beliefs, customs, practices, and social behavior of a particular nation or people.

entourage—A group of special employees who go with a high-ranking or famous person on visits and engagements.

epitomized—Was an ideal example or a typical sample of something.

frenetic—Characterized by feverish activity, confusion, and hurry.

genres—Categories into which artistic works can be placed based on style, form, or subject matter.

homage—A show of extreme respect toward someone.

mainstream—The ideas, actions, and values that are most widely accepted by a group or society.

marketable—To be suitable to be sold.

mastered—Recorded the original copy of something from which other copies can be made.

mixtape—A compilation of songs recorded from other sources.

negotiating—Attempting to come to an agreement on something through discussion and compromise.

notoriously—Relating to being famous for something bad.

oppression—The condition of being harshly or cruelly dominated by someone or a group of people.

protégé—A young person who receives help, guidance, training, and support from someone who is older and more experienced.

reggae—A style of music that originally came from Jamaica and combines elements of rock, calypso, and soul and is accompanied by a syncopated beat.

samples—Pieces of previously recorded sound that are used as part of a new recording.

underground—Separate from the mainstream culture.

venues—Locations for events.

Index

About the Author

A native of Philadelphia, Lindsey Sanna has worked as a professional musician and performer in both the United States and Europe. Her membership in the Rainbow Company, an urban theater troup, introduced her to the hip-hop aesthetic. She is currently completing a Master's degree in Education at Villanova University.

Picture Credits

Garces, Juan / PR Photos: pp. 8, 26, 32, 48, 54
Hatcher, Chris / PR Photos: pp. 24
iStockphoto: pp. 18, 40, 45, 53
    Hood, Eric: p. 12
    Klusacek, Milan: p. 31
    Medley, Bruno: p. 34
    Murat: p. 21
    Nehring, Nancy: p. 42
    Oanta, Flavius: p. 51
    Tzolov, Nick: p. 11
    Zivana, Ufuk: p. 16
Kirkland, Dean / PR Photos: p. 2
Tepper, Nicholas / PR Photos: front cover

To the best knowledge of the publisher, all other images are in the public domain. If any image has been inadvertently uncredited, please notify Harding House Publishing Service, Vestal, New York 13850, so that rectification can be made for future printings.